Hello Fiendish Followers,

It is with immense pleasure tha. ̄ ̄ ̄̄̄̄̄̄̄̄̄̄̄ to you the "Need," a captivating novella written by my dear friend, Gary Baker. As someone who has had the privilege of witnessing his talent and dedication to his craft and community at large, I am excited to see his work come to life within the pages of this tantalizing story.

Throughout "Need," Gary's masterful storytelling takes us on a thought-provoking journey, exploring the depths of human lust and power. With each chapter, he skillfully weaves together a complex tapestry of emotions, unveiling the innate yearnings that reside within the darkest recesses of all minds.

What truly sets this novella apart is Gary's ability to create a sense of relatability within the characters. Through their experiences, triumphs, and struggles, we discover the power of our own deepest desires and the lengths we are willing to go to satisfy them.

"Need" is not just a narrative; it is a reflection on the essence of humanity. It challenges us to examine our own desires, questioning what truly drives us and how far we are willing to go in our quest for fulfillment. As we follow Gary's characters in this transformative journey, we are led to confront our own truths and discover those universal longings that bind us all.

I hope you embark on this literary adventure with an open mind, prepared to be captivated by the power of Gary's words. Let "Need" carry you through a rollercoaster of emotions and leave you pondering the depths of your own desires.

Enjoy the thrilling ride that Gary Baker has crafted for us within "Need." It is my pleasure to present this novella to you and I eagerly anticipate the profound impact it will have on your mind and rhythmic blood flow to all your major organs.

With mouthwatering art provided by the superbly talented Danny Fisher you will undoubtedly feel the "Need" to serve your Queen.

Yours Truly,

# NEED

## By

## Gary Baker

Alexis wiped a hand across her sweat drenched forehead. The fire blazed through the toy factory and the blare of the alarms echoed through her panicked thoughts as she tried to make sense of what was happening.

Seconds ago, an explosion tore through the small factory, interrupting her routine at the assembly line where her quick, nimble fingers checked the dolls for defects before heading on to packaging. The blast, immediate and fierce, ripped through the assembly room in a flash of heat and pressure. The aftermath left overturned equipment and melted plastic dolls everywhere.

Alexis grunted as she gasped for the air that burned her lungs with each inhalation. Pieces of sanity broke through as she took in her surroundings. One of her arms was caught under the overturned metal belt, pulped in a mess of blood and flesh.

"I don't want to die," she said, her voice cracking like dry, dead leaves.

Alexis was stuck, pinned by the heavy machinery, and the slow realization of impending death crept across her flame blistering face. What was left to do but die before the shock wore off and the pain overwhelmed her, leading to a slow torturous death?

Cries reached out for help, for comfort and reassurance, but her voice would not join the chorus. Weak and raw, it rattled, and the fire heated breathes she had already taken were rushing her toward darkness. She felt the icy fingers of death squeezing her lungs and heart even through the searing air. Hot tears streaked from the corners of her eyes as she began to give up.

A minute passed in slow ebbing pain as her vision narrowed and the blackness of oblivion closed about its edges. A foot away from her she found her last focal point. The head of an Emma Doll, its plastic, raven locks already melted and one side of its tiny, clementine sized head melted until a nickel's worth of space had opened.

She laughed, hoarse and hacking, as the absurdity of a life wasted was reflected back at her through the tiny doll's disfigured head. It was fitting, she thought, to die staring at the ridiculous little toy she had wasted so many years of her life on assembling.

There was movement in the doll's head; the quick flicker of a snake-like tail, black and scaly.

"But how?" she railed. In these final moments it was the how that bothered her, not her imminent death. The heads were solid pieces of plastic. Fifteen years on the assembly line had taught her that much about the product. She could write it off to hallucination if, in fact, the movement was not escalating as it did now.

The tail vanished from sight and a small, leathery head emerged from the melted opening. A tar black, cracked tongue darted out and licked at the scorched air. And its eyes, red and alert, had fallen on her. A flurry of blurred motion confused her momentarily, and then it was there, clawing at her agape mouth and forcing itself down her damaged air way.

She would have screamed, if that was an option, but she was beyond producing sound now. If the strange little creature wanted to curl up inside her and die with her, then so be it. There was nothing left to fight for, so she welcomed the encroaching dark as it swept over her.

Her eyes flew open, and suddenly alert she moved, fighting against the belt pinning her down. She shifted on the floor, aware of the orange blaze consuming everything around her, and braced her legs against the overturned equipment. She could see her exposed skin blistering under the intense heat of the devouring flames. Suddenly she didn't accept death as the final answer. Gritting her teeth beneath her splitting lips, she shoved hard, and her arm tore free at the elbow leaving the ruined flesh behind to burn into ash.

Something's off, she thought as she stumbled toward freedom. She should be dead, but step by step, moment by moment, the increasing inferno caused her less pain, and her vision was clearing up. Looking down, she saw her clothes were tattered or burned off. One bare breast jiggled, exposed to the air with the plastic arm of a doll seared to the ample flesh. She reached up with her remaining arm and tore it free.

Her screaming pierced the factory, the only noise left besides the crackling of the flames and the crumbling of various objects being claimed by them.

She reached the north wall. Her body reacted before her mind could comprehend its actions. Her left leg shot out and kicked a hole in the wall, sending huge cement bricks flying off. She struggled to understand how she could be capable of such a superhuman feat, but the need to survive spurred her on and she squeezed through the small opening to the fresh air outside.

The morning sun mirrored the blaze inside and seared her with its bright assault. She went to cover her eyes with her right arm, but half of it remained inside. She raised her left, blocked the rays with it, and pushed forward, breaking into a limping run toward the forest, visible just past the parking lot.

*It's shaded there. It's safe there. We can heal there.*

"We?" she said, her voice returning, "Who the fuck is we?"

Alexis couldn't panic anymore, her body simply had nothing left and she collapsed just inside the wooded expanse, landing face first on a carpet of soft green moss.

A beetle crossed her plain of vision as for the second time her consciousness began to recede. She felt the faintest stirring of hunger spark inside, stirring her appetite. "So odd," she thought. Her jaw creaked open, charred muscles having trouble with the motion and her tongue, insanely long and split at the end, speared out and snatched the beetle. An instant later she heard the crunching in her head as she chewed. She passed out again before she could scream.

\*\*\*\*

*Wake up!*

Alexis was sprawled across her apartment's carpeted floor. Movement came hard. Something was constricting her attempt to rise and when she lifted her lids to see her surroundings, it was through a milky film.

She started kicking, realizing she was encased in some kind of cellophane type bubble, suspended in cream colored mucus. One kick, two, and finally a third and the bubble, at last punctured, released its contents. Instinct spurred her on and she slid down and out of the egg casing.

Coughing and scrambling, she pushed herself up with both arms and rose to stand in the muck of her rebirth.

"Wait," she said, remembering the explosion and the fire. *There had to be more.* The rest hit her hard, the memories crashing down, flooding her head like a burst dam and she knew what happened.

Fresh tears threatened, but she held them off and ran for a mirror, clutching the forearm that should be ash by now, left behind, a victim to the flames.

She shouldered open the bathroom door, desperate for answers. The cool tiles, slippery against her fluid covered feet, caused her to slip. Her scream never surfaced as her back collided with the floor, slamming the breath out of her lungs.

*Get up! Get up and see my gift to you.*

The voice again, clawing forth from the dark recesses of her mind. Calm washed over her, and she filled her lungs with the stale air of her apartment. The voice soothed her, an intimate friend sweeping the pain from her body and allowing her to stand again.

"Who are you?" she said, turning to peer into the mirror.

*My race is The Suppressed. We were damned for our sins, for satiating the Need we were born with, and then cursed in these putrid forms. We have crawled back over the millennia, and we will thrive once more. You are my vessel. Now I am yours and you are mine. That is all you need to know. Live with me or die without me.*

"I chose life," she said to her reflection, her humanity recoiling at the image. The fluid clung to her, warm and sticky, as if she had been dipped in honey. Her obsidian hair was slicked tight to her scalp, but it was her arm and face she stared at now. Her face was no longer scarred and blistered by the fire. Her skin seemed soft and smooth and the crow's feet and wrinkles that had creased her once vibrant beauty were gone. The dark blue of her eyes shone no longer, replaced by black rings and a red center, almost glowing, that reminded her of the inferno.

She raised her arm, spreading the newly grown appendage, splaying out her fingers while twisting her hand and then finally making a fist. She felt power like she had never possessed. A slow, full lipped smile spread deviously across her renewed features.

*Good girl. You will be the start of our rebirth and your reward shall be eternal life. You are whole now and very soon the Need will consume you as it has us. Together we are Queen!*

Alexis liked the sound of that, Queen. Her life had been hard and painful, bouncing from one abusive relationship to the next. But now she felt true power coursing through her veins and firing her soul. The painful aches of past abuses no longer throbbed in tear inducing reminders.

She started a hot shower, tracing her fingers over no longer existing scars, inside and out. The jaw that had clicked since being broke by an angry ex-lover was now strong and straight. He had hit her after he had failed to cum during sex, blaming her for his own inadequacies. And there were more from other relationships, a cut on her hip after barely avoiding being stabbed, the dull ache of broken ribs after being kicked and beaten, and a myriad of emotional scars from being told she was worthless and a whore.

They all washed away from her, fading down the drain, the hot spray cleansing her, body and soul, as the creature inside remade her into something more than what she could have ever hoped for.

With the cleansing, desire awoke, the first time in ages she had felt the hot flush of need swell her clit and invade her womb. She needed release this instant and sank to the soapy floor, shower head in hand and bracing her bent legs against the other side of the plastic tub. She twisted the head to a pulsating, steady line and, pulling her hood back with her free hand, directed the hard stream directly onto her clit. There was no build up, no steady throbbing into a shuddering orgasm. The release was immediate and wracked her core. The years of shame and abuse no longer holding her, and the years of frustration exploding behind her closed lids shook her. A primal, ancient scream, buried deep inside her exploded out and her legs, flexed against the weak plastic, convulsed until the thin barrier shattered and her feet disappeared into the wall.

"Damn, that was wonderful," she said, dropping the shower head. The sight of her legs leading into the wall caused a short fit of laughter and her breasts jiggled with the effort. "I don't fucking care about this place. It's just us girls now."

*Yes, and so it shall always be. Your release will not leave you satisfied for long. It was empty, meaningless. Soon you will gather what we need and you will understand our role here.*

****

Alexis lived in one of the four apartments the old house was split into. She had a view of the street and shared an entrance into the basement with the tenant of the other lower apartment. This place had been her refuge when she finally had decided to run and start a new life, but her luck had followed her here, to the small town of Harper's Hollow. Her life seemed stuck on repeat, move, get a shit job and shit boyfriend and then get abused. Wash, rinse, repeat…just like her shampoo instructions, only sad and pathetic.

"How long have we been here?" Alexis asked, already at one with the presence inside. She crossed to her window and drew back a curtain, peeking outside. She saw black smoke rising in the distance, from the toy factory where she worked. "It's still burning?"

*It's been six hours of your time.*

Six hours? Alexis reeled back from the window, shaken. It felt like days had passed and here she was alive in her apartment, recreated through the new life inside her. "My god, they'll be looking for me."

*Yes. It is not important. We will go and start the breeding. You will not want anything more than me, and to feed the Need.*

And it was true; she wanted nothing more than to feel the vibrancy of life coursing through her veins, the companionship of her new entity and the rising desire to fuck, breed and reproduce.

"Reproduce what? What am I now? What did I wake up in and how the hell did I get to my apartment?" The questions flew fast, speeding past her lips as soon as her mind formed them. How had she not questioned all of this yet? How much had changed in her? How much did she really care if they had?

*My species are the first life, the filth born from the excrement of the world as it was formed. We ruled and thrived until we became lazy, and man suppressed us, chased us back down into the earth where we lay, dormant and adapting until our return.*

*Now, you are more than you were, as too, am I. I don't exist in the form you first saw me in. I crawled into you, gave up my body and became one with you. We are power and purpose.*

"You brought me here?"

*Yes, and the changes I made allowed you to live. You secreted the fluid that formed the regenerative shell around you.*

Alexis stood in the center of her living room, seemingly talking to herself. It struck her how strange the image might be, but pushed it down, desperate for more answers.

She would have to wait. Sirens wailed outside and the screech of tires against tar could be heard on the street.

"Shit," she said, lurching into action. She leaped forward toward the door, punching out her newly formed arm, and blew it open. Seconds later she had descended the stone steps and entered the laundry area, a dimly lit room that reeked of mold and old sweat. The basement entrance lay in the back, past the ancient washer and dryer that rattled next to her.

Her neighbor, Martin, stood wide-eyed, in front of the dryer, forgotten laundry falling from his open hands.

"Alexis?" he asked.

"More or less," she answered, then grabbed him by the arm and dragged him, screaming, into the basement.

****

From upstairs Alexis could hear the knocking of the police on the front door. Being a solid piece of oak with a heavy bolt, it had no window. No window meant they couldn't see her ruined door. Still, she had the matter of Martin at hand.

He was squirming and trashing about beneath her. She crouched, huddled over him, one arm out and a hand, clamped like a vice, was locked over his mouth as he continued to try and scream. All his struggles, the thrashing of limbs and kicking of his legs, failed to budge her.

Instinct replaced thought and her new form, ever adapting, reacted for her. Cocking her head forward, she met his panicked eyes, brown flashes of color that darted in frenzied dashes.

"You must be calm, Martin. What I want from you is what you have always wanted to give me. So, stop fighting me, you can't win." Full, plump lips parted, and her forked tongue licked out, caressing the flushed cheek of her captive.

Her nerves started racing, starting a spark that became a current of hunger that overtook her senses. The forked tongue rose, wiggled wildly in the air before Martin's terror filled vision, and then split into eight snake-like tendrils. They danced wildly, like tiny snakes cut from the belly of their mother and allowed to spill out, sending chaotic lashes in every direction. The tendrils suddenly darted forth, splaying out over Martin's sobbing face. They swelled and pulsed once, covering the captive in a golden mist.

Martin passed out immediately, going limp beneath her. She wanted nothing more than to fuck him now and take his seed, but it would have to wait. Upstairs the front door was being pounded and Alexis knew she would be found out soon if she didn't run.

The back of the basement had several windows, made of glass bricks, and she discarded her captive momentarily and began punching through one of them. The glass cut her hands up, leaving long gashes that were already stitching themselves back together. An aggressive, angry growl passed through her tightly drawn lips, and she tore at the basements concrete blocks as well, creating enough space for her to escape through with Martin's unconscious mass.

"Downstairs!" The word echoed down, triggering her into action. In one leap she was at Martin and scooping him up in a clumsy embrace. She made the newly rendered hole in another focused bound and pushed Martin through before squeezing herself after him.

Her legs just cleared the hole when she heard the quick pop of gunfire behind her. Two more pops and a shot got lucky, ricocheting up and into her calf. She fell, screeching, inhumanly shrill, her leg on fire and already changing, becoming leathery and hard, a protective shell to ward off more attacks. The calf convulsed with the change, pushing out the bullet along with another screech and the officer that shot her made the error of poking his head out of the hole to see where his suspect lay, making his last mistake. She waited, clawed hand drawn back, and swiped at his throat, opening a canvas of blood and flesh where his throat had been moments earlier. She kicked out, sending his crimson spouting form crashing back into another officer that grunted with the impact.

*RUN!!!*

"I am, that fucker shot me!" Alexis gathered Martin back into her arms and jetted away from the horror she left in her wake. She hadn't wanted to kill anyone, but she held no regrets over it either. The world would respect her finally or there would be a price to pay.

****

The bed she set Martin on was crude, made of leaves and their discarded clothes. Almost an hour had passed, and her victim was just awakening, groggy and confused but with an erection that sprang toward the tree tops.

*Take him slow. The mist you sprayed him with will leave him enthralled by you. It is also working inside him, increasing his seed to impregnate you, making it stronger and more plentiful. Tease him, let it boil inside and beg for release and then take him and let him fill you. Kill him after or leave him, I care not which, but mate him now while his seed calls out to you.*

"Like I have a choice," she scoffed, "I have never felt so horny, so in need of being fucked."

Alexis crawled over to his stripped naked physique. She could smell the blood pumping through his cock; smell the pre-cum starting a slow dribble down his purple domed head. She needed to taste him, needed to wrap her tongue around his shaft and feel the blood pulsing through his thick veins, making him hard for her.

She crouched down, inhaled the musky scent of his cock, and extended her tendrilled tongue out, engulfing it in a many coiled grip. The split parts of her tongue milked him, passing up and down his shaft, pulling at his soft exterior and massaging the hardened muscle beneath. The tendrils danced, exploring every inch of his cock and then extending down to caress his rough ball sack.

Above her, Martins moans burst out in short pants, and she knew he was ready. She released his manhood, drawing her tendrilled tongued back inside her mouth and brought herself up to mount his prone form. There, in his glossed over eyes was all the approval she needed. He wanted her impaled on him, needed the soft folds of her pussy to slide his cock home into.

She hovered over his erection, her lower lips swollen and puffy, dripping the nectar of her loins down onto the purpled head of his cock. Never had she been this wet, needed cock as badly as she did now, and never had she taken one in this way. Her lips pushed out, sucking at the head briefly before she slammed herself down, accepting the full length of him inside her.

She knew her body acted differently, like an alien to her, but it had never sung with this much joy before. Her parts acted in their own way, adjusting to her needs and acting on her desires.

She bounced on Martin's cock, meeting his thrusts by slamming herself forcefully down on him repeatedly.

When his lips parted, she fed him her full breasts letting him suckle her nipples. She fed him more of her serum, keeping him impossibly hard and horny, through her nipples. Martin sucked hard, in need of her milky emission.

"Yes, Martin, give yourself to me. You are mine and I will feed your need to fulfill my own."

*He's close, take him deeper, accept his gift, and create our offspring.*

"Yes," Alexis said, thrusting her hips forward, sliding up his steely rod and bucking backward again, burying it deep inside her womb.

Martin began moaning into her tits and bucking beneath her, his orgasm racing through his veins, eager to sow his seed.

"Now, Martin, fill me."

They convulsed together, her release tightening her nipples and locking her pussy over his pulsing shaft. She could feel everything with her newly altered self, feel the throbbing of her sheath over his jerking cock and the spray of his hot cream spreading over her womb, spurt by spurt.

Over and over, she slid up and down, her nerves alive and dancing in ecstasy. Her milk had done its job, increasing Martin's release. She felt the excess cum flowing from between her legs, sliding out of her satiated pussy and out over his hard cock. She raised her hips up, letting Martin's dick pop free, excitement flushing her nude skin, and looked at the creamy mixture pooled beneath his balls, spreading over the bed of leaves.

"Thank you, Martin," she said. She bent down, laid a quick kiss on his nectar covered lips and left, leaving him naked and alone. She didn't want Martin dead. He was the only man that had ever been kind to her, so she left him there, smiling and happy and hoping when his mind cleared that he didn't start screaming in horror.

****

*His seed is already at work inside you. Your whole cycle will be a day at most, and in that time, you must protect our unborn until we can release them. You will feel on fire soon and it's best to find someplace cool and near water. Delivery in water is best. You are very special Alexis, chosen by us to be our queen, to be my vessel and equal. Together, we are resurrection, to ourselves and to our breed.*

"I'm special? So, what about the explosion, the fire, and the doll head you were in?" she said, and started running toward the toy factory and beyond to the large pond behind it.

*There are more of us out there, among you, but they are the workers helping us get a foothold in humanity. We are mainly female, the male of our species for breeding only. Most of my kind in the factory died in the explosion so we could find each other. The doll was my protection while I grew, until finally they laid me down on your line. The explosion had to happen in case our bonding failed. Our true forms cannot be discovered until birthing. Soon, ushered in by our offspring, our new day will dawn.*

Alexis ran, her energy never fading, but her core grew uncomfortably hot, a light flicker of heat blossoming into a full-blown blaze. Clutching at her stomach, she crumpled down, crashing to a skidding halt.

"Fuck, I feel hot, like fire is coursing through my veins and lava in my belly."

The spasms rocked her, hot electric shocks that knotted her muscles and seared her with pain. It happened so suddenly Alexis never noticed she had fallen in the clearing, just outside the blanket of trees. She was exposed and vulnerable, and every time she flashed her lids open, she could see the factory, the charcoal husk of her past, burnt and decrepit in its ruin, surrounded by police cruisers.

Her future burned in her belly, baptizing her in the flames of rebirth. The steady changing of her form unsettled her at first but the lightning-fast adaptations were proving addictive, wielding power she knew not the scope of, but engorged in fully.

The fire inside abated briefly, and she leaped up and sped anew toward the pond. There she could quell the flames and control her pain as her babies grew quickly inside her womb. She surged, desperate to be in the cooling waters before the next wave of heat overtook her. She raced along the perimeter, her legs lengthening with each stride, custom made for speed.

A loud sound echoed, and then another and a pain erupted at her side, along her ribs. She'd been nearly shot, a quick inspection showing a thin line of blood where she'd been grazed. She dropped to all fours, crouched for a moment as her torso elongated and her arms mimicked the shape of her back legs, ready for speed and clawed to wreak terrible vengeance.

*Do not let them stop you; do not let more men hurt you, hurt our offspring. Protect what is yours.*

"I fucking plan to!" The words came out hard and deep, her voice changing as her jaw widened and her teeth daggered.

Alexis turned abruptly and headed for the first cop she saw. He kneeled, crouched by his squad car, pistol steadied and taking aim, the distance of a half a football field between them. She covered it in seconds, darting erratically with each report of the gun until she collided with him, the force of the blow embedding him in the car door.

She cast her red eyes at him, fury boiling and then released, her scream the whistle of the kettle of her unleashed rage as she tore at him. He felt nothing, already dead, but her rage would not be abated until he was bloody piles or rendered flesh strewn about her clawed feet.

More shots punched into the metal behind her. A quick glance showed a group of officers, too many to count in a glimpse, closing the distance to her, guns at the ready.

She ran. She wanted to rip them all apart, but the fire was building inside again, and she needed to make the water.

The cops faded away, her speed too much to match. She passed the skeleton of the factory's docking bay and spotted the pond at the office park. Spectators littered the area, the kind of people that reveled in other's pain.

"This'll be fun." She spat the words, venom lacing her whispered threat.

The screams started immediately, a symphony of terror and panic rising into the unforgiving shadows of the descending eve. Nightmare had become reality and the bodies fell in a vicious wake of crimson as Alexis cut her way to the water. Two more bodies fell before her at the water's edge. She dove in, disappearing below the surface.

****

Coolness blanketed her as she made for the pond's deep center. Gills had already sprouted below her ears, behind her jawline, as she sank to the dark center. Only instead of complete darkness it grew brighter by degrees. The source of the light shocked her. It emanated from her growing belly, full and rounded now and glowing gold in the murky depths. Her rounded stomach rippled with the motion of a million writhing forms, agitated now in their need for birth.

Despite the cooling submergence, she twisted in agony as the heat spread from her womb. Their offspring were ready.

But there was a problem.

Splashes sounded around her, dull echoes returning from the top. They were not alone.

*Birth them and they will save you. The others are almost here and there will be more to come. Release our children, let them feed.*

"You told me I had a day," she said, thinking the words to the other.

*I am sorry Alexis. I was wrong. Our children are ready now. Will you deny them?*

"No, I won't."

Alexis screamed a muffled percussion in the watery depths as her womb expanded and pressure from her core separated her legs. Things were beyond her control. She felt her core split open and her legs spread to impossible angles. And then pain erupted, setting off fireworks behind her clenched lids as her offspring flooded from her womb, frenzied and starved. Alexis kept screaming, every fiber of her body being torn apart and remade as the birthing overtook her. Her red eyes glared, seeking out her escaping children as they spiraled up toward freedom and the surface to confront humanity.

They were beautiful, she noticed, long slender amphibian-like missiles rocketing upward to protect their mother and join with those deemed suitable. Their slimy little forms emitted the same golden hue as the mist she had spread over Martin. She fell back, unable to do anything but convulse in pain and watch her offspring flow from between her legs. Their journey would soon be complete, hundreds of little lives created by her to reshape the world.

No, not just her but the Other as well, joined with her soul and as much her as she was now. The Other's presence always felt, always guiding her, making her more than she ever had been. These thoughts ran through her mind as the last of her children swam to the surface. She watched, the other inside seeing through her, but not trying to control her, letting her enjoy her new self as she had from the start.

And so, she lay flat on her back and exhausted on the bed of the pond as the rapid healing process began. It needed to be quick; her children would need her soon to lead them. The stitching of her insides, rebuilding of her joints and realignment of her being came as rapidly as the birthing. Necessity fueled change and she finished her transformative healing, accompanied by the loud cracks and pops of reformed sinew and bone, the blistering pain becoming expected now, and ignored, the next stage of her evolution upon her.

****

Topside, around the pond, the world had forgotten Alexis and discovered terror in her absence. People ran amok, wild and hopeful of their pending escape, only to be confronted by the harsh reality of despair as they succumbed one by one to the lizard-like racing beasts that had risen from the still waters.

The little, fast-moving creatures emitted the golden mist like steam in a sauna. It rose from their darting forms and hung in the air, transfixing the men. The lucky ones died, the potent vapor too strong for their systems to absorb while the remaining men stood, dazed and obedient, waiting for their queen's command. Subjugation was total and with the takeover came the need to shed their clothes and bare themselves to the women, naked and erect with their varied members bobbing in the air, dripping shimmering pre-cum from cock to ground.

The women were scared, their screams forever silenced as their agape mouths were entered and the children of Alexis slithered in, clawed limbs prying their jaws wider to accommodate their invasion. The change, immediate and total, seized them. They collapsed as the joining took place, one life melding into another to make one whole entity, new and old and with a singular purpose. The last stage of the birthing neared completion and the women rose. Their eyes, like their Queen's, were red and angry and sought out conquest. Already, they moved forward, toward the men and knowing they must feed their need.

The area from the pond to the outskirts of the factories was littered with writhing bodies as the mass mating began. The women took the men, now their slaves, and descended upon the hardened cocks, licking and preparing as their tendrilled tongues serviced all the stiffening flesh. Nectar giving nipples fed suckling lips and soon the grunts and moans of the unnatural orgy echoed into the night sky.

One man emerged from the forest, blind in his obsession as he sought his mate, his Queen. Martin raced through the entangled lovers; his senses peaked at animal awareness. The smell of sweat and cum excited him and engorged his own erection further. Since his first mating with Alexis it had grown impossibly long and swung between his legs, the bulbous head almost brushing his knees.

**\*\*\*\***

She could feel him, even submerged beneath the weight of the water, and she knew her chosen mate approached the pond's edge. An impossibly wide grin split her new face, spreading from one jaw joint to the next in a tear of flesh, and she flashed upward with renewed vigor. In seconds she broke the surface and ascended the cool spring air.

The leathery beat of wings perked her ears. She looked over her shoulder at her flapping appendages.

"So fucking cool," she said, floating like an angel of death above the orgy. "Martin."

*He is ours now, forever. When you left him alive his connection became complete. You will mate with him again and the children we have will rule this world one day. You have evolved, the prime form of what you are.*

"What we are!" Alexis stated firmly, indicating her and the creature. She caught her reflection in the water, a dark mirror lit by the full moon.

She looked like herself again mostly, wings and split face aside. Her skin appeared soft and feminine, but she knew it was like iron, hard and impenetrable. Her ample breasts swayed and leaked, the nectar dropping like tears in a still pool.

*Yes, what we are. Now let us go to him, breed him for our master race, and we shall show man a dawn born under a blood red sun.*

Alexis swooped down, a dark angel descending triumphant, and shouldered Martin to the earth.

"On your fucking back Martin!" she hissed.

Martin obeyed, incapable of doing anything but serving the wishes of his Queen. He turned onto his back and presented his cock to her, hard and straining to be buried in her waiting womb.

"Yessssss, Martin." Alexis lowered her hips, his oversized cock stretching her moist lips open and then filling her completely, one glorious and agonizing inch at a time. Her sheath surrounded and gripped his steely length, excited by the full feeling of his hardness.

Again, she fed Martin her nectar, pushing her distended nipples to his eager mouth as he thrust inside her slick walls. She knew the nectar would hasten his release. She needed that now with the shrill blare of sirens announcing the imminent arrival of reinforcements. She would have his seed by then and be pregnant.

Her life from now on would consist of ruling and birthing. The painful first birth now completed, she would cycle birthing after birthing, and watch as her children became one with the women of the world.

Below here Martin convulsed as his cum exploded from his mushroomed head, bursting out in great excess from his slit. Alexis saw the lights pulling up and stopping, but she waited the last few seconds until Martins gift was dripping out and trailing down her thighs. Now, they would pay for coming here.

Before she could engage the oncoming officers, the spent men that had risen from their mating's were in motion, their one goal to protect their Queen. Their fierceness, wild and untamed, unleashed in savage brutality, ripped through the approaching police force.

Some of the Queens protectors fell in the onslaught of bullets loosed by the officers, but not enough to matter. The echoing screams of the dying men, and regrettably some of the uniformed women, delighted her ears but trouble loomed. Two Police cruisers were pulling away.

*We must stop them before they escape. They can make trouble for us. We need time and the blanket of anonymity this town provides.*

"They won't get far," Alexis said, rising into the air once more, the beat of her leathery wings flapping like laundry pinned up in a wind storm. The cruisers quickly came back into view as she rode the air current, staying low and keeping her eyes locked on her targets.

Alexis swooped down, landing on the shoulder to the road leading out of the factory's parking lot. Two rocks half her size laid, one on each side, framing the exit letting out to the main road. Hefting one high, no more work than lifting an egg from a carton, she narrowed in on the first cruiser's windshield and threw with all her rage. Her muscles twisted, knotted and released as she brought the large stone above her head and then threw it.

It flew, like a speeding missile, straight at its target. Seconds after leaving her steely grip, the windshield of the first patrol car shattered, blown out by the deadly projectile. The rock passed through the thick glass like a bullet through gauze, pulping the driver and ending its journey lodged in the backseat, painted crimson and peach with the remains of its victim.

The ruined vehicle spun in the following cars path. The collision could not be avoided, and the second cruiser slammed into the driver's side of the first vehicle, filling the night with the rending crunch of metal.

Alexis counted four officers, alive and dazed, making their way from the carnage of their cars. One female and three males, two of the men badly injured. The metallic taint of spilled blood filled her head, distracting her, bringing her hunger to the forefront.

The Queens children arrived in time to see their mother feeding on the two most injured men. She held the other two survivors, one in her right hand and the other trapped beneath her left foot, writhing on the cool pavement. Her head snapped down and the throat of one officer disappeared in a spray of scarlet. A second snap tore a gaping hole in the second injured man and all that remained of his chest was a pool of meat and blood. Their last breaths were behind them, their eyes dead and blank, as their flesh fed her hunger and their crimson flow sated her thirst.

"Yours, my children," Alexis said through her blood red maw, dropping the woman from her outstretched hand, and raising her leg to free the trapped man. "Bond her and breed him. This town is our new breeding ground."

Alexis looked out over her children, a mother overseeing her young, and enjoyed the scene before her. Some were still fucking and collecting cum deep in their wombs, preparing to birth her army. The air reeked of death and sex and the burnt carcass of the factory.

"Thank you for finding me. Thank you for making me a god."

*It is as it was fated to be. You know what we must do now.*

"Yes, so shall it be."

****

The next day.

"The fucking town seems dead," Sheriff Alden said over his radio to base. "I'm looking for anything I can see. If I don't find anything out in the next few minutes be ready to take this higher." The Sheriff placed the mic back on its clip and rolled slowly through town. The streets were bare except for red blotches that too closely resembled blood to him. Homes were open and doors and windows torn asunder. It looked like the town had suffered through a massive hurricane or worse.

He could have sworn someone had tried to contact him a few hours ago from Harper's Hollow. No, he knew someone did. A lone scream had pierced the static and interrupted his drive-thru dinner. He worked on occasion with the officers here and felt obliged to check up on them after he failed to raise them through the radio and phone.

Tingles ran up his spine, like an ice cube being slowly drawn up his back. Outside his window some hope finally came into view. Things still weren't right though. The mall was packed with vehicles. They weren't parked so much as left in various places and odd angles. Something here stunk of trouble and sweat beaded his creased brow.

"Things are damn creepy here, George," he said after retrieving his mic. "All the cars seem to be at the mall here. Looks like a bunch of damn women parked them. Do you copy?"

"Base hears you loud and clear, Sheriff. Just be careful over there now. You see trouble; you call it in right away and we'll get help on the way."

"Will do, George. Just gonna have me a quick peek inside and see if there's some kind of emergency meeting or somethin'," Sheriff Alden said, suddenly feeling hot and flushed, dampening his uniform in his cold sweat.

He parked his car on the road and started toward the mall entrance. He walked slowly, peeking into and at the cars strewn about the parking lot. It seemed unnatural, more like they were dropped in place instead of parked. The puzzle didn't make a whole lot of sense and he hoped inside the small mall held some much-needed answers.

"Almost to Harpers Mall entrance, George. None of this makes a lick of sense. Haven't seen or heard a damn thing since arriving." He mopped his forehead with the sleeve of his uniform, mic still firm in hand. "Wait, I can see movement inside and…. Oh Fuck…..ahhhhhhh."

The glass doors shattered, and the sharp shards punctured Sheriff Alden's face and torso. His scream ended when the claws of the horror before him punched through his neck. His head bobbed to the side and the mic fell from his dead hand to hang at his side as the creature carried him inside.

**\*\*\*\***

The inside of the mall bustled with the scurrying movement of the nest. The Queen sat high on the second story on a throne of dirt and twisted steel. The mall, now hers, served as her lair and the breeding ground for her army. The men, cocooned to the ground with hard cocks raised to service the females, moaned in ecstasy as their rigid members dripped their cum in ample supply.

Martin approached, carrying the sheriff's lifeless bulk and she beckoned him forward.

"What is it, Martin?" she asked, reaching down and running her clawed fingertips from his balls to the leaking tip of his crown.

"Exactly what you wanted my Queen," he answered, shutting his eyes and enjoying her touch.

The mic on the dead man came to life. "Sheriff Alden, you there? Sheriff Alden? Fuck, I'm sending back up sir."

Alexis shot her tongue out like a razor-edged whip and severed the coiled line, silencing the radio.

"Come, Martin," Alexis said, guiding his stiff cock toward her open slit, "We must have more offspring to greet our impending company. The world is ours now Martin, and no longer will our kind be repressed by men. A new order has arrived. Now fuck me, Martin. Breed me so I may cleanse this world."

Alexis laughed as Martin's cock entered her, certain in her victory. In time all women would be bonded and all men their breeding slaves. The world would be perfect.


The End

Made in the USA
Coppell, TX
05 February 2025

45503144R00022